Challenge in the Dark

Mike Baxter's first day at a new school marks the start of an unforgettable week. From the moment he comes face to face with the dreaded Steven Taylor and his brother Spotty Sam, Mike is heading for the biggest challenge of his life.

Mike's friends 'help out' by setting up a dare for him – before he has time to protest. He then finds himself exposed to real danger, experiencing fear and panic, before he emerges triumphant and heroic.

Challenge in the Dark

ROBERT LEESON

Illustrated by Jim Russell

Tameside School Libraries

Lions

First published in Great Britain 1978
by William Collins Sons & Co. Ltd
First published in Lions 1979
Sixth impression August 1990

Lions is an imprint of
the Children's Division, part of
the Harper Collins Publishing Group,
8 Grafton Street, London W1X 3LA

Printed and bound in Great Britain by
William Collins Sons & Co. Ltd, Glasgow

For Catherine and Fred

Contents

Mike Baxter says:

"If your friends get you
    into a mess,
Your enemies have to
    get you out of it."

I

The Best of Enemies

Monday morning. Dad came yawning up the stairs as I came yawning down. He was coming off night shift ready for a good day's sleep. I was starting my first week at the big school. I'd have gladly changed places, but they don't take you on British Rail at eleven.

We dodged about on the stairs trying to get past each other. Then he said:

"Do your best, Mike."

"OK, Dad."

I did my best, too. Before my first week at the new school was over I had two nightmares, a black eye and was nearly trapped ten feet underground. But I'm telling this too fast. Back to Monday.

Mum was in the kitchen. Our Sis had rushed off

to work early for some strange reason. So I didn't get any sarky remarks from her. That helped.

"Have you got your dinner money?"

"Yes, Mum," I splurted.

"Don't talk with your mouth full, love."

"Yes, Mum."

"Have you got your plimsolls?"

"Yes – No, Mum, have I heckaslike. We don't need them today."

"Don't swear."

"Heckaslike isn't swearing."

"I don't like it anyway."

"All right, Mum."

"Have you got your key? I may be out when you get home."

"Yes, Mum."

Mum came along our road and down Station Road with me. Then she turned off along High Street to the offices where she goes cleaning. She wasn't thrilled about that but she had to do it. That's how I felt about the new school.

Mum gave me a kiss. I sneaked a look round. There were some kids on the other side of Station Road, but they didn't see anything. I don't think.

"Look after yourself, Mike."

I whipped across the road by the station and walked along by the shops. I wanted to get a fun-sized chocolate bar from the newsagents, to keep my strength up till break time. Fun-sized. They mean small. Why can't they say so?

The shop was packed, but I couldn't see anyone I knew from our old school. That was the trouble. My mate Ranji wasn't coming up till next year. He's six months younger than me, though you can't tell. My other friend, Sandra, is thirteen and she doesn't go to the comprehensive. Her Dad sends her to St Winifred's. He thinks it's a good influence on her and we're not. Fat lot he knows. Anyway, he's away from home half the time and she's got no Mum, so she has to look after her brother Andrew. He's a pain, Andy, only eight, but big as a baby elephant. And everywhere we go, he goes. Like it or lump it, says Sandra. So we lump it.

But I wouldn't see any of them till the weekend. Baxter man, you're on your own for the week. And didn't I know it.

Before I realized, I was in School Lane, pushing about among a big crowd of kids, all my own age. The older ones were coming in later, so we had the big school to ourselves for the morning. They call it the big school – well, because it's bigger. Everything's bigger – the yard, the buildings, the stairs, even the teachers. And as soon as we all got into the yard, this voice came over the loudspeaker system.

"Wha-ha-haw-haw-hoo-hoo-ha," it went.

"Eh, what was that?" I asked a lad standing next to me.

"Do not resist or you will be annihilated," he answered.

Very funny.

I could see this place was going to be dodgey. Instead of staying in one classroom all the time, you trail round with your gear from one place to another.

And in each room you get a different teacher. Where do they get them all from? How can you tell them apart? I began to panic. But then we were all called into the assembly hall and sat down. I could see one or two people I recognized now, but they were farther away in different groups. I was in 1J.

A teacher at the front started talking to us. I found out afterwards he was The Voice – the one who made those weird noises over the tannoy. But he sounded almost normal right now.

He rambled on about the school, how it used to be a grammar until they changed it, so that anyone could come there.

"Oh ah, even nits like Baxter."

What was that? I could hear somebody having a giggle behind me and sneaked a look round. I didn't fancy what I saw. About a row back was someone

from our old school, with one of his mates. He was
Steven Taylor. I knew him all right – and I wished
I didn't. Steven Taylor's thin and pale, and his face
is like a ferret's with a sharp nose and red eyes.

I'd run across him more than once – trying to get
at me, needling me for one reason or another. I
could take it in the old school because I had my
mates. But here I was on my own. And just my luck
to have him and his mates in my class. This *was*
going to be dodgey – I could feel it.

Still this school was a big place. I'd just have to
keep out of his way. I pretended I'd heard nothing.

The rest of the day went quickly and I began to
get the hang of the school, where the assembly hall
was, where the dining-hall was, where the labs were,
where the lavs were – even they were bigger.

They let us out at three o'clock that first day and
I got into School Lane smartish. I passed cocky
Steven Taylor nattering to his friends, showing off.
In fact he was so fond of the sound of his own voice
he didn't even notice me. I shot off up School Lane
and into Station Road. Steven Taylor lived near
the railway and I lived farther up the hill, near the
Park. So, once I was over the railway bridge I was
on home ground, more or less.

That day I was in luck, because Mum was home

after all. She'd got off work early and was busy at the cooker.

"How did it go, lad?"

I flopped down at the table.

"Is that fish fingers, Mum?"

"Get your coat off, wash your hands and I'll tell you."

"Ah, it's fish fingers, I can smell it."

"The lad's a genius. That's modern education for you."

My sister, Laura, came barging in through the kitchen door. I blew her a raspberry.

"Education's wasted on some people," I said.

"Give over, you two," said Mum. "Somebody put the kettle on."

Our Sis disappeared. She's crafty. I filled the kettle at the sink and Dad came into the room, half asleep and rubbing his eyes.

"Now, Mike, how did it go?"

"Oh, all right, Dad. Hey, it isn't half big that place."

"Ah, think you'll like it, Mike?"

"I think so."

Mum put the fish fingers in front of me. I remembered I was hungry – only a chocolate bar and a fun-sized school dinner since dawn. The fish fingers were hot and burned my tongue as I swallowed.

"Aaargh," I said.

"Manners you pig," said our Sis, coming back into the kitchen. She put on a posh voice. "Is that what they teach you at Bugletown Comprehensive?"

"Oh, get—."

"That's enough, Mike," said Mum.

"Ah, let's have a bit of peace," said Dad, pouring out the tea.

When we'd finished eating, Dad put the telly on. I sat there watching and feeling comfortable. Then I remembered Steven Taylor.

Well, I thought. I'll just keep out of his way. It's a big place, after all.

But I was wrong. It wasn't quite big enough.

2

A Close Shave

The rest of that week I got my own breakfast because Mum went to work early. Sometimes I had our Sis for company, if you can call it company. She's as bog-eyed as me at that time in the morning. But at least I don't get any sarky remarks. In fact we leave each other alone. I say nothing to Mum about her eating with a magazine propped up in front of the marmalade pot; she says nothing if I stick my breakfast between two rounds and rush off down Station Road with it.

Fried egg's just right if you do it on both sides; bacon's OK if you take the rinds off. Sausages you have to press flat between the slices or they jump out at the sides. Scrambled egg's a dead loss, and I ask you, what can you do with a cornflake sandwich?

I began to get really organized. Wake up when Mum calls me as she sets off for work. Turn over and have twenty minutes more kip. Wake up again when Sis bangs on the door as she goes to get her cat wash. Ten minutes more, then stagger up, have a quick refresher with a damp flannel, not too wet in case I catch cold. Then, into the kitchen dressing on the move, make my mobile breakfast. Five minutes later I hit Station Road.

That week I kept on the far side of Station Road. It meant staying out of the shops and missing my fun-sized chocolate bar. Still, who needs chocolate bars when they have a well-pressed sausage sandwich? At the bottom of Station Road I went across like a rocket into School Lane, mixing with the crowd like a man on the run. Then, through the gates and into 1J for registration. Mr Jackson would say, out loud on purpose, "Aha, Michael, let me guess – hamburger this morning?"

And I'd say, just to be friendly: "How did you know, sir?"

"Because it's still in your ear."

What a comedian

Mr Jackson has us sitting round the room in alphabetical order and because I'm Baxter that means I'm as far away from Steven Taylor as I can get, unless I swap places with Chris Adjei. Break times were tricky, but there's one good thing about a big school – it's big. There are plenty of places to tuck yourself away when you want your own company – or don't want someone else's. And I found out something about lunch break. Mr Jameson in the Biology Lab, likes help with the animals. So I would slip into the lab after my dinner each day. What better way to spend a wet lunchtime – and keep out of other people's way? And, useful too. If I fail my 'O' levels I can get a job mucking out hamsters at the zoo, perhaps even work my way up into the big time with the elephants.

It all went like a dream until Thursday. In fact I'd almost forgotten Taylor. But on Thursday, at break time, when I was going across the yard on my lawful business, I saw a big crowd over by the lavs. I couldn't help it, I just had to see what was going on. It was a fight, two big blokes punching each other like maniacs and blood flying.

"Hey, are they sixth form?" I asked somebody at the back of the crowd. He looked at me and laughed: "Get off, they're fourth years." Fourth years – that big? It made me feel smaller still. Just then, one of them got it right on the button and there was a big cheer. It made me feel funny inside and I thought I'd go somewhere and sit down. I turned round and pushed my way out of the crowd which was getting bigger.

"Who do you think you're shoving?"

Oh, Nora. There was Steven Taylor right in front of me.

"I'm not shoving anyone."

"What do you think I am, the Invisible Man?"

That got a laugh. Some of the crowd gathered round and blocked my way, worse luck. Then I noticed who was standing behind Stephen Taylor. No wonder he was so cocky. I'd forgotten he had a brother in the fourth year.

Sam Taylor, Spotty Sam they call him – big, broad, thick as two planks and nasty with it, something from Outer Space.

"Look," I said to Steven, trying to pretend I hadn't seen Spotty Sam, "I wasn't pushing you." I dodged to the right, but another bloke got in my way.

"He's shoving everybody. He's a bully. Bully Baxter, the Terror of the First Year. I say, chaps, let's tell teacher."

They're bad when they're nasty, worse when they try to be funny. And it wasn't funny to me. I didn't want to fight Steven Taylor I don't know why, I just didn't. But I couldn't get away.

"Go on," said Spotty Sam to his brother. "Poke him one."

He did. At least he started. But, without thinking, I got my fist up in the air, just at the same time as his. They met, 'klonk' and we both hopped around holding our hands. Knuckle on knuckle, the pain was fantastic. I thought I saw a way out and was just going to love them and leave them, when somebody pushed me from the back and I went flying into Steven and he went flying into big Sam. Sam pushed his brother back, but I'd moved and he went flying on to the ground. When he got up, he was livid. He went bananas. "Aaaarghle," he said and went at me like a tank. He got me one in the eye and one below the belt.

"Kill him," yelled Spotty Sam, and I think he meant to, but just then, we heard:

"Wha-ha-haw-haw-hoo-hoo-ha-ha."

The tannoy was going. Everyone looked round. Except for about five of us, the yard was empty. I was saved by The Voice. The Taylor brothers and their mates walked off. Steven, really cocky now, looked round.

"Right. Baxter, you can order your coffin."

Charming.

3

Granddad's Story

I was in a tight corner. I wasn't going to get myself caught at the school gate by Taylor and his heavy mob – at least not before I'd had a crash course in karate and kung fu. I had to make a getaway when school ended. But the classroom was arranged so I was farthest from the door and Steven Taylor was nearest. Though if it came to the push I reckoned I could beat him in the 100 metres dash.

While Mr Jackson was dismissing us, I got my stuff together under my desk, looking straight at him as though I was listening very hard to what he was saying about something we needed for the next day. But who cared about tomorrow? Today was enough for me. I pressed down with feet and hands like a runner waiting for the starting gun and the second Mr J. stopped talking I was away across the room like a rocket. Taylor stuck his foot out, but I gave his ankle a sideways tap (as shown on 'Match of the Day') and nipped out sharpish. I could hear Mr J. shouting: "Come BACK, Michael," but I kept going.

I didn't take a breath until I was half way down School Lane. And I was turning into Station Road, when I suddenly let out a yell that made all the old ladies waiting at the bus stop, give a jump. I'd just remembered. Dad was having a day off and Gran and Granddad who live in the old people's flats up at Penfold would be at our place for tea. Wa-hey! I could hear the old ladies going on about how that school had gone to the dogs since it went comprehensive, but I couldn't stop for a discussion. I burned up Station Road and when I landed home, they were all there, except Sis who isn't very keen on family teas.

Granddad was well away. Not drinking, I mean, just excited. He gets carried away when he tells one of his stories. His face is usually pale and grey, but it gets all red and often he can't speak for laughing, and then he coughs and chokes and our Gran has to bang him on the back till he gets his breath back and he wheezes for about ten minutes. But there's no stopping him. As I came in through the back door, I could see him in the front room, bouncing up and down on his chair and making the tea things rattle. He was waving his arms about and doing aircraft noises, so I knew he was on about The War. I went and stood in the front room doorway, listening.

"He was sleeping down there when it started. Jerry came over on the way back from Liverpool, and was dumping bombs near the low level line . . . and the walls in those shelters were shaking . . ."

"They never were safe," interrupted Gran.

"Who's telling this? He woke up. He thought it was a nightmare. He'd dreamed he was down the pit and they'd all gone up to the top and left him. He jumped like a scalded cat when he heard the bombs whistle. He knew he'd had it if he didn't get out . . ."

"What have you done to your face?"

"Eh, what's that," said Granddad, looking at Mum, who was sitting on the other side of the table holding up the best teapot. But Mum was looking at me and now they all turned and stared. Gran got up and came over.

"Whatever have you . . . ?"

Granddad started to laugh again.

"He's been in the wars, that's what . . ."

"You be quiet," said Gran. She put her fingers on the side of my face. I jumped.

"That'll swell up tomorrow. Here, love, come in the kitchen and I'll give you something to put on it."

Gran opened the fridge and got out some raw liver.

"Here, hold that on your eye."

"Get off," I said.

"Don't be daft, now. Hold it on. It'll draw it out."

The liver felt cold and wet. But my face stopped tingling. Gran was fishing around in a carrier bag. She whispered.

"Some of my fudge here. Not a word to your mother, eh."

"Don't give him too much, our Mum," said Mum from the other room. Gran shook her head. Then she raised her voice. "You miss nothing, do you, our Betty. Can't think where you get it from."

"Not from our side of the family," said Granddad from the front room.

"A right argumentative lot I married into," said Dad. "Come in here, Mike. Let's have a look at you."

They all stared at me as I went into the front room. Mum wasn't pleased. I could see.

"What about the other bloke?" asked Dad.

I shrugged. I couldn't tell them the other bloke didn't even have a mark on him and I was scared stiff he was going to fill in my other eye when I got to school the next day. I mean, there are certain things it isn't good for parents to know. I thought I'd change the subject.

"Can I have some tea?"

"You can wash your hands, first," said Mum. But she was smiling. She always liked it when Gran and Granddad came round, even though they always argued the toss. I liked it too, and not just for Gran's fudge, which is the greatest, but for Granddad's stories about The War, or when he was down the Pit. Though it makes me feel a bit funny when he gets excited and starts to cough and cough. Mum doesn't like that either, I can see.

I sat down at the table. I left the bread and butter and started on the cakes. For once Mum didn't seem to notice. I wanted to hear more about that bloke trapped underground. It's weird how you want to listen to something that puts the wind up you. But they'd changed the subject.

Gran was going on about some trouble with their pension. But after a while they were quiet, so I got a word in.

"Hey, Granddad, which shelters were you talking

about – those on the main road, opposite the Three Fiddlers?"

"What's that, Mike, lad?"

"Those shelters, where that bloke was buried . . ."

He stared at me.

"Them? They closed them down. Never were safe. Death trap they were."

"Yes," said Gran. "They ought to be filled in. You remember when those two little boys were missing. They found them down one of those tunnels. Nearly suffocated they were. Lucky to be alive."

"That's right," said Mum, looking at me. "You keep away from there."

I spluttered.

"If you don't mind, I was only asking Grand-dad . . ."

"Don't talk with your mouth full."

You can't win.

Later that night, when Dad was going to drive Gran and Granddad over to Penfold, Gran took me on one side.

"Here you are, love." She gave me a 50p piece.

"Now, listen," she went on. "You keep out of fights. It won't do you any good. You get on with your school work. I wish I'd had a nice school like that when I was your age."

She gave me a kiss.

Granddad punched me on the arm and slipped a 50p piece into my pocket.

"Listen, Mike. Just give him one between wind and water and when he doubles up, get him one in the eye. You'll have no more bother."

With all that good advice I couldn't go wrong.

I don't know if it was Granddad's story or an old film I watched just before I went to bed, but I had a nightmare. I was in an underground tunnel, pitch dark. And something was after me. I tried to run, but my feet were caught in giant cobwebs. It came nearer and nearer. I could hear it breathing.

Its footsteps went Thump, Thump, Thump.

4

On the Run

Thump, thump, thump.

"Wake up genius."

Sis was banging on my bedroom door. Where was I? I rolled out of bed. The covers were all over the floor. What a night. What day was it? Friday. Late for school. Who was I? I looked in the mirror. Gran's treatment had worked. My eye looked like a piece of liver now. Still it wasn't sore any more. Just my good looks were ruined.

"Who is the greatest?" asked Sis, who was in the kitchen burning toast when I got there. I took no notice and looked in the fridge. There were some pilchards left over from tea the day before, so I got those out. A bit cold on an empty stomach, but I didn't feel up to cookery that day. I wrapped them in foil and stuck the packet in my bag and trundled off to school, my feet like lead. Who knows, I might have to hide out in the boiler room all day.

But things went well at first. Mr J. greeted me with his usual charm and wit. He must have forgotten my crash exit yesterday. Then I had another bit of luck. They were showing a film to the lower school about things a healthy boy or girl ought to know. You know, one of those films where the audience thinks they know it all already. Then there was a talk and it lasted so long it took up most of break. I caught sight of Taylor once or twice, through my good eye. He looked so pleased with himself it was sick-making. Near dinner time somebody passed me a note. It said:

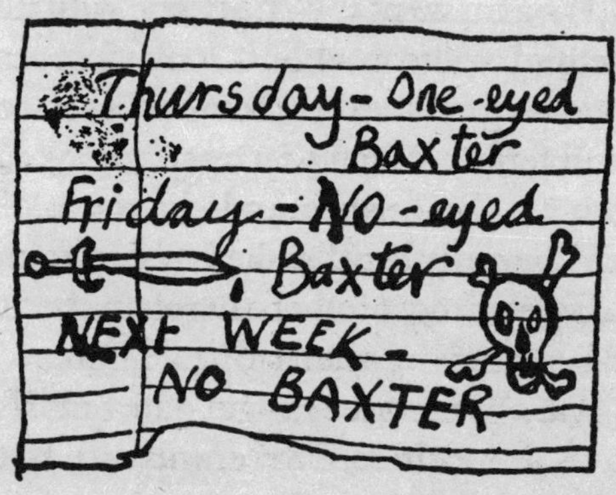

But I got through dinner time by good management. I went straight from the dining-hall to the Biology Lab and spent a pleasant time with the white rats. Except that one of them had a face like Steven Taylor.

Mr Jameson told me the rats were being kept for dissection by the 'A' level people.

"What's dissection?" I asked.

"Cutting up," he answered. For a **moment** that cheered me up. Then I thought, don't be horrible, Mike, taking it out on that poor little rat. Just because it looks like Steven Taylor. Come to think of it, it didn't look like Taylor at all, in fact it was quite good looking. I put my hand in the cage to stroke it and it bit me. Maybe it was Steven Taylor, after all.

The afternoon went by a bit too quickly for my liking. We had a lesson about early times in Britain. The only thing I can remember was something about blood feuds. When you get done, your brother has to wait in the bushes and do the bloke who'd done you. Then his brother has to get your brother, till they all get tired of it or there's nobody left. To think, these were grown people, too. The big question was, who would get Steven Taylor? I didn't have a brother. There was Sis but I don't think she was interested in blood feuds. From her remarks about my face this morning, it was all a bit of a giggle to her.

Of course, there was my mate Ranji and Sandra and her little brother Andy. They'd stick up for me. But they weren't around. I wouldn't see them until Saturday. Every Saturday morning we used to meet at the old oak tree on Barker's Bonk, at the top of the park. It's a funny old tree, hundreds of years old, they reckon. But instead of growing right up, it sticks out from the Bonk – sideways. When we meet we sit on the branches way up above the ground. Ranji sits farthest out, then I sit farther in, then comes Sandra, and Andy's nearest to the ground. We do all our planning there. Tomorrow, I thought, I'd tell them all about my aggro with Steven Taylor. They'd know what to do.

The point was – this was Friday. How did I reach Saturday? The history lesson was ending and this was the last period. I got my gear together and when we were dismissed I didn't make a dash for it.

Mr J.'s beady eye was on me and I realized he hadn't forgotten about yesterday. He was playing it cool, waiting to see if I'd try it on again. The thing was – what was worse – Mr J. or the Taylor Mafia? I sneaked a crafty look round at Steven

Taylor's desk. There was no one there. He'd gone. My luck was holding.

Come on Mike, I told myself. Up School Lane, over the road, up the other side of Station Road, across the railway bridge and you're home and dry. And, tomorrow's SATURDAY. Ho ho.

Ho ho.

They were waiting for me at the school gate – Steven Taylor, Spotty Sam, Gary Wilson and one or two more. I went cold inside. I could feel the pilchard lying wet and heavy on my stomach and wished I'd taken the bones out before I swallowed it.

Then I had a brilliant idea. I kept on the pavement on the same side as they were and walked brass-faced right up as though I was going to walk in between them. That got them. They couldn't believe their eyes. Just when I was a few feet away I suddenly dodged out into the road and round them, lashing out with my bag at the nearest one as he tried to get in my way. It hit him a right thump, I don't know where, but I didn't care, because I was doing a high speed gas down the Lane dodging in and out of all the crowds going home. As I crossed Station Road, I could hear them behind me.

"Give up, Baxter. Make it easy for yourself. It won't take long."

I didn't wait to find out what 'it' was. I put on pace up the rise in Station Road, towards the railway. Maybe Dad would be coming off work just as I got to the bridge. Correction. Dad was on nights and tucked up safely in bed. Not much use.

I panted up to the railway bridge. The Manchester train was going underneath and it let off a big shriek and a cloud of grotty smelling diesel fumes as I ran by. I took in a big breath right then and nearly choked.

I felt sick. It slowed me down right when I needed my strength, because the road runs uphill from the railway, past the park and on to Penfold. I took a quick look back. I couldn't see them behind me, so I slowed down and got my breath back.

"Baxter, you've had it."

Oh no. They were on the other side of the road, the side where our street runs in. They'd been crafty and cut me off and now they were almost level with me. There were only three of them, Steven, Spotty Sam and Gary Wilson. The others weren't interested in duffing up Baxter. But three were quite enough for the job. I took another deep breath and put on some more speed, pulling away from them, though still on the wrong side of the road. What could I do? I couldn't run all the way to Penfold where Gran and Granddad live. That was six miles.

Without thinking I crossed the road. Maybe I could get down a side street and work my way back into our road. Over my shoulder I could see them, the Taylors in front and Gary Wilson behind. I started to turn into Bishops' Road, then almost too late, I remembered, it was a cul de sac. I'd be trapped.

Right in front of me now were the park gates. I'd no choice. I ran in, cleared the flower beds with one leap and ran on up the slope. In the back of my mind was the idea I could get to the top of the Bonk where there was more space and dodge round them. But I was running out of puff and I began to slip on the grass as the ground got steeper.

"Come on, we've got him now," Steven Taylor was yelling.

I'd reached the foot of the Bonk and the old oak tree was above me, its branches and leaves shaking in the wind. My breath was nearly finished and my chest was sore from running. A stitch in my side almost creased me. I stopped and doubled up to ease the pain, as they came puffing up. I took a good grip on my bag-strap and swung it round.

"You've – had – it – Baxter." They were nearly finished as well. But they came on stumbling up to the Bonk and looking mean. I was going to get done.

But just as they were nearly on me, someone shouted, "Come on, Mike. Up to the tree. Come on!"

5

At Barker's Bonk

"Come on Mike," the shout came again. And at the same time, down from the top of the Bonk, by the old tree, came a shower of clods. One hit Steven Taylor smack in the face. That improved his looks no end. Another one got big Spotty Sam on the side of the head. Gary Wilson didn't get his because he was too far down the slope.

I started scrambling up the Bonk. At the top I could see my mates. There was fat little Andy pulling up another clod. Behind him was Ranji, grinning a big grin, and Sandra, in that grotty green uniform they make them wear at St Winifred's.

Spotty Sam saw them too.

"Hey, come on," he yelled. "There's only a Paki and a girl and a little kid."

Oh, he shouldn't have said that. They all came off the Bonk like a tornado and before Spotty Sam knew what day it was, he got Sandra's hockey stick, thin end, right between wind and water, as Granddad would say. He grunted and rolled over down the slope. Steven Taylor decided to pull back to safer ground and Gary Wilson, who was farther down, started to look as though he wasn't with them.

"Is that what they teach you at St Winifred's?" said Spotty Sam, when he got his breath back and climbed to his feet. He wasn't badly damaged, because Sandra hadn't really used the stick the way they do on the hockey pitch. But I could see his pride was damaged. He started to climb back up the slope.

"You come up here, and I'll give you the other end somewhere else," said Sandra.

He stopped. She meant it. He knew.

"Anyway," she went on, "what do they teach you? Three on to one?"

"What can you expect?" said Ranji. "The ignorant pig doesn't even know the difference between India and Pakistan."

Sam Taylor started to say something, but changed his mind. He wasn't quite sure what Sandra would do next. She's tall for thirteen and even in that weird green uniform she can look quite tough. The three of them stood together at the foot of the slope and looked at us four, standing together half way up. We had the advantage and they knew it. Steven Taylor wasn't talking so big, now, and I began to feel better.

"It wasn't three on to one," said Spotty Sam. The funny thing was, he was trying to sound reasonable, as though he wanted to calm Sandra down.

"Well, it looked like it to me," said Sandra.

Steven Taylor said his twopennorth.

"Him and me were going to have a fight and he ran away. He started it."

"You lying—" I began to say, but Sandra waved her hand at me.

"Who says he has to fight you, anyhow? It's stupid, chasing him all the way up here. Haven't you got better things to do on a Friday afternoon?"

They couldn't see she was being sarky. Sam got bold again.

"Look, it's got nothing to do with you. My brother's going to poke him one, and he's going to get it. If he doesn't get it now, he'll get it on Monday, back at school."

"Oh ah, all you lot on to him," said Ranji.

"No, just the two of them."

"How do we know?" asked Sandra. "If we

hadn't been here, you'd have all been on to him."

Sam looked crafty. You could see his brain creaking.

"OK, then. Let's have it now. There's three of us and four of you. My brother and Baxter can have it out and you can see we won't touch him."

Oh oh, I thought. Spotty Sam can get really dangerous when he starts using his brain. Sandra didn't say anything. She couldn't really, because there was nothing wrong with what Sam was saying. Sam grinned. What a sight.

"Of course, if he wants to hide himself behind a bird, there's nothing we can do, is there?"

"Ah, he's chicken," jeered Steven. "Let's leave him. We can get him on Monday and give him a real doing. He can't bring her to school with him." He started to giggle. "Please teacher can I bring my girl friend to school with me. Steven Taylor's going to bash me and he makes me cry."

I was so mad all of a sudden, I could have gone down and started on him. Well, almost, but Ranji got hold of my arm.

"My mate's not interested in fighting your little brother, Spotty Sam," he said.

"You watch it," said Sam, but he had one eye on Sandra and he was listening. Ranji went on:

"Thumping people's easy. But what about something that takes real nerve. Something Mike's got and your little brother hasn't."

"Come on then," said Sam. "Tell us. We know he can run. What else can he do?"

I stared at Ranji and so did Sandra. Who was this Mike Baxter, Ranji knew? I'd never heard of him.

"My mate," said Ranji, "can go down the shelters and stay down there. I bet little Steven daren't. Mike can go down and stay down all day. He's not scared."

"Ah, get off," said Steven, "there's nothing in it." But he didn't mean it, I could see.

"All right," said Ranji. "Have you been down?"

"Hundreds of times," said Steven.

"Right," said Ranji. "Which way did you get in?"

"Ah – from the main road," but Steven wasn't so sure.

"Liar," said Ranji. "There's no way in from the main road. It's all boarded up and locked. Go on, admit it, you've never been down."

"Neither have you," said Sam. He was guessing now.

Ranji grinned. "No, I haven't, but I know how you get down. There's a way in over the back.

"The boards are loose and you can crawl through if someone holds them back for you."

"Hey," said Sandra, "that means once you're in, you can't get out again."

"Hey," added fat little Andy. "You could be stuck down there for ever, underground."

"That's right," said Ranji. "But Mike doesn't care. He'll go down, if you go down. And we'll all be outside and see who chickens and wants to come up again, first."

I started to say something, but Ranji kicked my ankle.

"Come on then, Sam." Sandra had caught on. "What does your little brother say? How about tomorrow? Let's see who's really got nerve. I bet it's really creepy down there."

She was getting to Steven, I could see. He didn't like the idea. But what about me. Who said I liked it. I nudged Ranji, but he took no notice.

Sam kept quiet a minute, then, "OK, Agreed. We'll meet you on the main road opposite the Three Fiddlers, tomorrow, at ten o'clock."

Steven looked sick – like I felt, but he couldn't say anything. Any more than I could. The three of them began to walk off slowly down the slope towards the park gates. Sandra shouted after them.

"You can bring one more, same age as our Andrew, to make it even. See you tomorrow."

6

Ranji's Brainwave

I stared at Ranji, dumbstruck.

Sandra put her arm round my shoulders.

"Poor old Mike. He'll never recover. He never knew how brave he was."

"Very funny. With friends like you lot, I don't need enemies," I snarled.

"Ooh, Mike. You never said that when we stuck up for you just now," squeaked fat little Andrew.

"And you can just belt up."

"Hey, Michael Baxter, don't you take it out of my lovely little brother."

Ranji began climbing back up the Bonk. "Let's get up the old tree again and talk it over."

As soon as we were settled, each of us in their

favourite place, and I got my breath back, I asked Ranji:

"Just what did you reckon you were playing at down there? My mate can do this, my mate can do that. You see what you've landed me in, now."

He shrugged. "What did you want, Mike? Anyway, it worked. It wiped the smile off that nit Steven Taylor's face. I tell you, he's dead worried."

Sandra nodded.

"What about me, then?" I demanded. "I'm dead worried, too."

"Well, you wouldn't fight him, would you?"

"I've got one black eye, already, thank you very much."

"So, what're you going to do, keep on running away and hoping he'll get tired? Look Mike, as long as Spotty Sam's around, Steven's going to carry on needling you. It makes you look small and it makes him feel big."

"So?"

"So, get him down the shelters, underground in the smelly, grotty dark, with earwigs making nests in his collar, and put the wind up him. So, then he'll leave you alone."

"But, Ranji, what about me? Listen, I know about those shelters. My Granddad was telling me the other night. A bloke was trapped down there

when the bombs were coming down during the war
– buried alive. I bet he's still down there. And our
Gran said two kids were lost down there once and
nearly never came up again and that's why it's all
boarded up."

While I was talking I could see Andrew's round
face getting paler and he shifted along the tree
trunk to get closer to Sandra. She looked thought-
ful.

"Mike's got a point, Ranji. It is risky. And how
do we know Mike's going to stick it out longer than
Steven Taylor? Wouldn't he be better off going
down to school on Monday, giving the little twit a
poke in the nose and then see what happens?"

I couldn't tell whether she was taking the mickey
or not so I said quickly, "Can't do that. We've
agreed to meet them by the shelters tomorrow
morning."

"Well, give him one on the nose as soon as we meet
them, then."

Ranji began to grin like a Cheshire cat. I know
that sounds daft, but that's what he did. He
scrambled along the tree trunk to where I was
sitting and slapped me on the shoulder.

"You know Mike, there's something about those
shelters which I know, but Taylor doesn't. Something my cousin told me."

I stared. "What's that?"

"Just inside the entrance there's a passage that runs into the middle. At least I think it does, but it may be blocked where the side's caved in. Anyway, just about twenty yards from the entrance, there's another little passage to the right. It's like a little cave, really, it doesn't lead anywhere. And if you get in this place, and look up, you can see out. There's like a shaft that goes up to the open air."

"Well?"

"Well, when you go down there, tomorrow morning you hide in the little side place. You'll be OK there, because you can see daylight at the top. You can stay there for hours.

Ranji was right. I began to feel better. The way Ranji had worked it out I had nothing to worry about – much.

Sandra saw my face, and laughed.

"You're OK, then, Mike. All you have to do is let Steven Taylor go in first. He'll get sick of it and want to come out and then in you go and make him look small. We can even tell their lot, we'll go off home for dinner and come back for you in the afternoon."

Before I could answer she jumped up.

"Hey, Andy and I have to go. See you tomorrow, by the shelters."

We all went off home. I was late for tea and Mum was a bit annoyed. But I felt in a better mood. Our Sis stared at me.

"What do you know? He actually likes school. Wonders'll never cease."

But I ignored her. I was beginning to feel good. Tomorrow I was going to make Steven Taylor look sick. Roll on tomorrow.

I felt good until I went to bed. And then I had another grotty dream, like the one I had the night before.

Something was after me, chasing me down this dark tunnel and I couldn't get away from it. And I knew what it was after me – it was that bloke who'd been caught down the shelters during the air raid. I struggled so hard to get away that I woke myself up. It was still dark and my heart was going like a hammer.

It took me hours to get back to sleep again.

7

Underground

I woke up, bog-eyed at half past nine next morning. At first I thought – right on, Saturday, and turned over again. Then I remembered. I jumped out of bed so quickly it hurt and rushed downstairs, got something to eat and was out of the house before I could even see straight.

I heard our Sis saying: "Isn't it marvellous. Mid-winter and he goes out without his jacket. Mid-summer and he wears that sweater. The lad's losing grip."

But I wasn't daft. I reckoned it would be freezing cold and damp, down those shelters, as well as dark and creepy and – why was I putting the wind up myself?

Before I knew where I was I found myself in

School Lane, near the school gates. I must have turned right from Station Road without thinking. I could just hear the town hall clock in the High Street start to strike ten as I got back on the trail and I skidded to a halt on the main road opposite the Three Fiddlers, just as the clock finished striking.

The shelters are on a big patch of waste ground just off the main road, with grass about ten feet high and even some hawthorn and elder trees. The ground is all lumpy and here and there are funny brick and iron funnels like a ship, sticking up out of the bushes, half covered with creeping plants. I was going down under there this morning and I couldn't help shivering a bit about it. The funny thing is, it made me think of Granddad. He went underground every day of his life and not just five feet or ten feet, but hundreds of yards.

The fence round the shelters was broken down in one or two places and I easily found a gap to squeeze through. Our lot were there already, little Andy jumping up and down, Sandra in tee shirt and jeans (I bet she was glad to get out of that green outfit) standing on a big grassy mound looking round. Ranji was squatting nearby looking as though he did this sort of thing every day of the week.

Sandra waved: "We thought you weren't coming."

Ranji got up and came over. "Hi, Mike. Look, quick before the other mob come, stick this in your pocket." He handed me a reel of nylon fishing line.

"What's this for?"

"When you get inside, fasten it to something. Then reel it out and hold on to it till you reach that side passage."

"But you said it was only twenty yards, there must be two miles of line here."

"I know, just in case of emergencies."

"Stop cheering me up. What emergencies?"

"You never know, you could lose your way."

Sandra jumped down from her lookout post. She slipped me a small packet in greaseproof paper.

"Peanut butter sandwich. Just in case of emergencies."

She was grinning. Little Andy pranced up and stuck a sticky lump in my hand.

"Half my chocolate bar, in case of e-germencies."

I pushed all the gear into my back pocket and looked up and down. I couldn't see Taylor's mob anywhere.

"Hey, perhaps they've given up," I said hopefully. But Sandra, who had climbed up on the hump again, called out. "They're just coming across the main road."

My stomach turned a bit. Ranji punched my arm lightly.

"Remember Mike, twenty paces in, on your right. You'll be able to feel the gap in the wall with your hand, you can't miss."

"Right – you said left, yesterday."

"Don't be daft, I said right."

Steven Taylor, big Sam and Gary Wilson climbed through the gap in the fence.

"Where's your fourth man?" shouted Sandra.

Steven Taylor grinned. "We don't need four. One of us is worth two of you lot."

That's funny, I thought. He looks cocky again. I wonder why. I soon found out. They stopped about ten feet away. Maybe Sam Taylor thought Sandra had her hockey stick hidden somewhere handy.

Ranji spoke. "Right. We'll toss up for it. Or your man can go in first, then our man'll go down as soon as yours gives up screaming, say ten seconds."

"Very funny," said Sam Taylor. "No, we've got a better idea." He was smirking. "Your man goes in first. We watch to make sure he goes right in. Then our man goes in and looks for him. As soon as he finds him, they swap over. The one who keeps hidden longest, has it."

I sneaked a look at Steven Taylor. He was fiddling with something, which he pushed back into his pocket, when he saw me watching him. What was he up to?

"What's wrong with our way?" I asked.

Sam looked crafty. "Anyone can go in there and lie low just inside and wait. That's dead easy. But going right inside and hiding while somebody else is looking for you, then hunting the other bloke, that's different. You need real nerve for that."

I whispered to Ranji.

"Hey, Steven Taylor's hiding something. Bet he's got a map or something. Let's make him turn his pockets out."

He whispered back. "Don't be daft. Suppose they make you turn your pockets out?"

"But this way, I won't be able to stay in that side place near the entrance."

"Yes, you will. It goes a way back from the main passage. Get in there and look small. Ten to one he'll never find you." Ranji raised his voice.

"All right. But our man goes in first. And if yours gives up, he's won."

Steven started to say something, but Sam nudged him and whispered. "OK," said Sam. "One go does it. Your man goes first. Come on."

Sam led the way on to the top of the shelters. The grass was thick and tangled up with nettles and brambles. We tripped and stumbled in little pits and bumps. It must have been about a hundred yards across.

"Hey," said Sandra, "they must have got thousands down here during the war."

"Twelve hundred and fifty," answered Sam. It was funny how polite he was to Sandra.

"Get off, how do you know?"

"Our Granddad was in charge of these shelters. He had to be on active duty when the bombs were coming down," he bragged.

So that was it. That was why Sam Taylor wanted to change the rules. He knew all about these shelters. Their Granddad must have given them a plan or something. No wonder Stephen looked so cocky. I looked at Ranji. He'd guessed what I was thinking.

"You're all right," he whispered. "You've got the line and food. You can stay hidden for a week."

Thank you very much.

"Here we are," shouted Sam, who'd gone on ahead. Hidden among all the grass and scrubby bushes, was a door. Really it was just some thick planks with creosote on and a big bar across with a padlock.

"We'll never get in there," Sandra said.

Sam jumped down into the dip in the ground in front of the planks and beckoned. He and Steven began to pull on one of the side boards. It was loose and began to come away from the others. Sam started to sweat and puff.

"Give us a hand, you lot. No not you, Baxter. You get ready to nip in there."

There was nothing for it. I got down on my hands and knees. The grass was wet and slippery. There was a gap about a foot wide between the planks and the earth. A stink of something rotten came out from the darkness underneath.

"Get in," snarled Sam Taylor. "You chicken or something."

I cringed myself together and crawled into the gap. My hands touched wet mud and my stomach jerked inside me. Someone gave me a shove with their foot (I bet it was Steven) and I fell forward, rolling over down a little slope.

There was a thump behind me as the planks went back. It was dark now, heavy dark, worse than night time. It was a thick, rotten, smelly dark and I felt dizzy and choked.

I was stuck underground, on my hands and knees on my own. I was right inside my own nightmare.

8

In the Dark

Still on my knees I stretched my hands out in front of me But I could feel nothing. The darkness seemed to cling to my clothes like fog. I started to panic and called out. My voice was squeaky, the words wouldn't come out properly. Then I realized I was facing away down the passage and the planks were behind me, so I worked my way round carefully, till my foot hit something. That must be the wall of the passage. Then I felt something else, solid and rough against my fingers. That must be the planks. Very slowly I got to my feet and leaned on the door, though I still couldn't see it. They reckon your eyes get used to the darkness, but this was so thick I couldn't see a thing, like being wrapped in black cloth from head to toe.

"Have to get a move on."

Who was that? It was me, speaking in my own head. Only it seemed to echo, as if my mind was a big room. I tried to get Ranji's fishing line out of my back pocket, but my fingers were shaking. Then I remembered I couldn't use the line, because they'd changed the rules. Steven Taylor would find it and pick his way along it. Have to go on without it. I swallowed very hard, three times and took a deep breath. (You always get dizzy if you hold your breath too long.) The air was full of this dead, stale smell and I choked. But I had to breathe. So I put my back against the planks and tried again.

Breathing in, I put out my hands to the side this time. Now I could touch the walls, easily. They were slimy, slippery and something crawled over my fingers. I jumped like a shot rabbit. Another three deep breaths to calm down and I started edging my way along the right hand wall. Ranji did say *right* hand, didn't he? I'd gone three steps before I remembered to count. Ten paces he said. My hand touched something thick and wet, that crumbled under my fingers. More deep breaths until I worked out what it was, a wooden post holding the earth wall up, like the pit props Granddad told me about.

I thought about Granddad then, walking along underground every day, just as though he were going down Station Road. That made me feel better. So I moved faster, though I still couldn't see a thing. You can *feel* darkness, though. I started counting again, seven, eight, nine, ten, eleven. Now I was getting the hang of it.

There was a sudden tearing noise behind me. I wished my heart would keep still. Then I knew – they were pulling open the planks to let Steven Taylor in. So I moved faster, twelve, thirteen, fourteen. There was no side entrance. Ranji had it all wrong – or his cousin did. What should I do?

Right at that moment, my hand went into nothing. The wall had gone. I waved both arms about, and then I found it again. This was the side passage, though it couldn't be more than two feet wide. And ten paces from the entrance – nothing. Ranji's cousin must have size twenty-nines on his feet. I'd just stuffed myself into the narrow gap, when I heard Steven Taylor's voice.

"Give up Baxter. You've had it."

I pushed farther into the gap. It got narrower and narrower until I could hardly move forward. I looked up, but it was pitch dark. I couldn't see whether I was on my head or my feet. Ranji's cousin didn't only wear size twenty-nines. He was a rotten liar. There was no daylight up there.

I pulled back several steps in a rush. I couldn't stand being in that tiny gap. It was like wedging yourself into a coffin. Then I saw light, a wavering light. But it wasn't overhead. It was down the main passage. They'd cheated, leaving the planks open for Taylor. But how could they – our side wouldn't put up with that? And that light was moving – coming nearer. Hey, the dirty – he had a torch. That's what he had in his pocket, a torch. He was more scared than I was.

Before I could stop myself, I shouted:

"Taylor, you crummy—, you had a torch."

I bent down and pulled up a lump of clay from the ground threw it as hard as I could. The light went out. I jerked back into the gap again, pushing right into the earth, till I could feel the slimy touch of it on my face and hands. Taylor came stumbling down the passage. He could have a taste of the dark now.

"Baxter, I'm going to get you."

But his voice was all funny and shaky. The sound came nearer. There was the light again. He needed that torch. The beam flashed in my hiding place, lighting up the soil and the wooden posts, grey-black and yellow where the edges had been knocked. Now he'd see me. I jammed myself as hard as I could into the end of the little tunnel as the light grew stronger.

The tunnel end gave way. I pitched forward, falling down, into nothing.

9

Nightmare

I landed with a thump, the breath going out of my chest, and lay still, my face stuck into wct, soft earth. Everything was black around. There wasn't a sound. The darkness in this hole was thicker than ever and the smell was even grottier.

My hand struck wood – planks standing up. I ran my finger along it. That was funny. It was a table, a trestle table, like Dad had in our basement to do his do-it-yourself on. I felt better right away. A table can't do you any harm. There might be chairs, as well, I thought – and a sideboard, and cupboards and a cooker. I started giggling. Drop in for tea some time. I'd fallen into someone's secret hideout. But whose? I stopped giggling and pulled myself up by the table.

My hands slid along the top and knocked on something. There was a tinny sound. My fingers touched metal, small and round – a mug, and a basin next to it. My fingers slipped inside the basin and jerked back of their own accord. The inside was all soft and mushy, like cloth or leather gone rotten. It was weird.

My knee knocked hard on more wood – a three-legged stool. Sitting down I began to run my hands along the table top again. A bottle. The smell from it was like nothing on earth – whisky or beer gone bad. Somebody had made himself comfortable here. But I wasn't. I had to get out somehow.

I stretched out my arms again. There was nothing. I stepped away from the stool following my arms. One step, two, three. I fell headlong. Not quite, for my hands struck the wall. My feet were all tangled up in something. I kicked and struggled but couldn't get free. Gritting my teeth, I felt down my legs. They were caught in some rotting old cloth heaped up on the ground. Somebody had left his clothes here as well as his mug.

My head began spinning round. Granddad's story about the man trapped underground came back. My nightmare came back. But now it was for real.

"Steven, Steven", I yelled. But my voice didn't seem to carry more than a yard. There was no answer, no sound. Nothing. "How can I get out?" I could hear my own voice. It was trembling as though I was going to start crying. Stumbling round, both arms out, I knocked up against the table. It rocked about. I gave it a pull and it came free.

I jerked at it with all my might. "Come on you—," I kept saying as I tugged and pulled on it and dragged it over to the side of the hole. I heard the mug and the old basin thing go sliding and clattering off as I slammed the old trestle so hard against the earth wall, it jammed back into my stomach and knocked the breath out of me again.

Now I clambered on top of the table so fast that my head and shoulders were crammed up solid against the wood and earth above me. That must be the top of this cave, or dugout thing. Somewhere there must be a way out, where I came in. Behind me came a slithering noise. It could have been a mouse or something, but I didn't wait to find out. Gasping and swearing, I scrambled like a drowning man trying to get up a river bank, scratching and scrabbling at the loose earth round the gap where I'd fallen through earlier on.

I lost my grip and slid backwards, banged on the table top and stamped hard to get going again. I clawed my way up again and then I was clear and into the narrow hole, fighting my way through the gap, falling forward, scrambling up, tripping over, falling down, getting up again, staggering into the main passage. If there was anything still down that hole it wasn't going to get me. Now I was running and running till I ran full tilt into the planks at the end of the passage, gasping for breath. My chest was sore and my shoulder began to hurt where I'd fallen. I had to get out.

I kicked on the planks and shouted, "Sandra, Ranji." No answer. I banged with my fists. I kicked again. But it was like hitting the side of a house. It hurt me and did nothing else. I even tried shouting "Andy" and then "Sam" and "Gary". If any of them had come, I'd have kissed them, starting with Sandra and even including Sam. But they didn't come. They couldn't hear. They were sitting up there, waiting for Steven to find me or give up.

For all I knew, Sandra and Ranji and little Andy were taking the mickey out of Taylor's lot, because they thought I was winning. I must have been down here an hour at least. Winning? I gave up shouting because my throat hurt. I gave up thumping and kicking because my fists and feet hurt.

I tried to think straight. There was only one

thing to do and that was to find Steven Taylor, even if it meant giving up. He had a torch anyway. He had a torch, and maybe if we got together we could push those planks back and get out.

Just then, as I was muttering to myself, I remembered Ranji's fishing line. There must be about a hundred yards and more on that reel. If I fastened it on the planks here, I could walk right to the other side and get back safely. I wasted no more time, though it was easier said than done, for the planks were tight packed together and I couldn't find any nails. But in the end I found a small split in one plank and threaded the knotted end of the line through that and pulled it tight.

This time I didn't feel my way along the walls. I walked straight ahead. I was beginning to get used to the dark again and it made me think of Granddad. When I got out I'd have a talk with him about it. Then, I thought again, maybe not, because if Gran heard, then Mum would find out and I'd be in trouble over-ground as well as underground.

So I walked ahead and the line reeled out behind me. In places I tripped up, and once I put my foot in a hole and ricked my ankle. Once I dropped the line and had to crouch down on the ground and feel around for it. When I picked it up again my breath went out in a great gasp. Don't do that again Baxter. I marched on. The other side must be near here, I felt sure, but I couldn't see anything. Then I stumbled and fell on loose earth, like a slope in front of me. The main passage was blocked. I poked here and there but the earth fall had closed it all up. But where was Taylor? What was he doing? Was he hiding somewhere and waiting for me to show up?

Well, I didn't care. I had to go back. This time I went along the wall, winding in the line around my fingers, and every now and then I felt along the earth and the posts for side passages. After about twenty yards I found one and explored down there as far as the line would take me. It was wide and there were spaces on either side. Was this where people hid when the bombs were coming down? It must have been weird during the war. I couldn't understand why Granddad made such a big joke about it. Maybe that comes from being older and looking back. But I didn't want to think too much about that because it brought that grotty hole with the man's clothes lying in it back into my mind.

I found another passage. But that was blocked up. The earth had come down. Suddenly I had a cold feeling in my stomach.

"Steven," I shouted. "Taylor, where are you?" But I got no answer. I worked my way back to the main passage, reeling in the line and pressed. There were no more side passages in this part of the wall and then I was back by the planks again. I pushed up against them and tried to find a crack I could see through. But it was no go. What were they doing up there? What were they playing at? We'd been down here an hour and more.

I felt hungry then and wished I'd had more breakfast. I thought about Sandra's peanut butter sandwich. Good old Sandra. I put my hand in my pocket to get it out. But it was gritty with dust and stuck together with Andy's chocolate bar. Eeyuch!

I had to keep moving. Where was Taylor? I tested the end of the line. It was still tight, so I set off along the passage again, this time keeping to the other side, going slowly and feeling for side openings. The first one I came to, my stomach gave a great jump. That was the gap where I'd fallen through. I hesitated a moment, then thought I heard a scratching noise down there, and hurried on again.

Another side passage, but this one was blocked up. The ground must have sagged in all over the place since the war. Or maybe it was the bombs. No, that was daft, I told myself. Bombs would make a big hole at the top.

At the next opening I went in. It was long and

narrow and at the end there was a cross tunnel. I tried the left hand side. I kept going and calling as I went "Steven, Steven". I must have gone a good fifty steps before I realized what had gone wrong. The line coiled round my fingers wasn't pulling any more. It was slack, the end had pulled free of the planks.

Now where was I? I turned round and ran back – ten, twenty yards. But there was no turning. I'd gone too fast. I must go back slowly, feeling along the wall. But which side? If I'd turned right first of all, the opening must be on the left. But I'd gone back on my tracks so which side was it?

There it was! No, that was on the wrong side. Should I try it? By now I didn't know whether I was coming or going, I stopped to try and think. There was a left turn from the main passage, then a right. Then I'd gone back and couldn't find the left turning, but I'd found this one on the right. I must go down here, but keep on looking for a left hand tunnel. But slowly. My chest started to jerk. I was holding my breath again. I let it go, breathed in, counted to ten, breathed out and in again. My heart beats went faster, then slower. They seemed to be outside my body. My throat was dry. I wished I'd brought something to drink with me. I'd been shouting so much my throat was sore.

I'd been shouting all right. But Steven Taylor hadn't been answering. The more I thought about it, the weirder it seemed. He was supposed to be looking for me, wasn't he? Here was I blundering about up and down all these tunnels shouting "Steven, Steven" and he wasn't answering.

Suddenly it hit me. Crafty Taylor, with his torch, had found another way out. He'd chickened out and left me down here. But if that was it, why didn't our lot come down and let me out?

I started to run again, not thinking where I was going, slipping and sliding on the tunnel floor. I ran slap into the end of the passage so hard I thought my head would come off my shoulders. I turned back and ran the other way, like a hamster in a cage. Now I found another turning and ran down that. I hadn't a clue which way I was going, where the main passage was, if I was heading north, south, east or west.

And all the time I was hearing this strange noise up in front of me, like someone hitting a tin can with a stick. I stopped. It stopped. I must be off my trolley. Then it began again, thump, thump. The funny thing was, it sounded as though it was outside, not underground. Hey up, there must be a way out, or something, this must be where Taylor got out.

I fell into an earth fall, but it only half blocked the way and I struggled over it and rolled down into a deeper passage. On my feet again in a flash and I was running – bang into another wall.

But no, it was a turning and – what was that – light ahead.

Come on Baxter.

10

Where is Taylor?

The light came down into the tunnel from above and I soon saw what it was. But there was no way out there, just one of the ventilation shafts I'd seen sticking up from the ground above the shelters. They were shaped like funnels on a ship I remembered.

Now I was underneath, standing in the patch of light just as if I was sunbathing. It was terrific – light. I could see the side of the shaft, brown earth and metal with some weeds growing out of it, and when I put my head on one side I could even see a bit of sky showing outside the slits at the top of the funnel. If I could get up there, I could see out.

It wasn't all that difficult at first, because the shaft had lots of cracks and holes in it. When I climbed up to the funnel part, that was harder, because it was only a foot or so across. But I managed to get my fingers into one of the slots at the top, where the light came through and hauled myself up. I wedged my toes in a crack in the wall and by twisting round I could see out over the top of the shelters.

Then I let out a great yell. About twenty or thirty yards away, under a bush growing out of the top of the shelters, were the lot of them, sitting together like long lost friends. There was Ranji, showing Gary Wilson a bit of paper. I bet he was trying to explain the difference between India and Pakistan to him. And there was Spotty Sam trying to chat up Sandra. Even from this distance she looked bored. And little Andy – what was he up to? He was bending down grubbing up bits and pieces from the ground. But what for?

I found out soon enough. He straightened up and gave a big jerk with his arm. The next thing I knew there was a clang on the side of the ventilation funnel that nearly burst my ear drums. He was chucking clods at it, and he was spot on.

"Hey, Andy, give over. Tell them to come and get me out."

Thump. He threw another one and it splattered soil through the slots on to my face.

"Andy, you stupid—" I shouted, chewing dirt and feeling sick.

"Sandra!"

"Sam!"

It was no good. They couldn't hear me. At least not with that bombardment going on.

"Hey!" I yelled. "Hey!" They took no notice, and my arms were ready to drop off with the strain of holding up to the slots.

"Hey—." Thump. He got another direct hit. I was showered with muck, my foot slipped and I fell crash down the shaft and rolled over on the ground about ten feet below, ricking my ankle as I landed. The pain was like fire for a moment and I had to sit and rub at it hard before I could get to my feet again. I could have cried, or sworn, I was so choked. I could have done both. I would have done both if I hadn't pulled myself together. I had to use my head. When I'd been looking out from the ventilation slots, I could see the main road. And I could see the other side of the ground, the back of the shelters where they'd let me in.

I stood up and held my arm out like a pointer. The opening with the planks must lie back the way I had come and over to the right. I'd make my way back there, taking it steady and just hang on until they came to let me out.

And that's what I did, but carefully, keeping the main direction in mind. A right turn, a left turn, then another right turn to put me on the right track again. I began to think about Granddad again, working along, underground, talking to his mates, perhaps having a swig of cold tea. That reminded me I was thirsty.

As I reached the main passage, it came back to me. When I looked out of the shaft I'd seen them all. But there was no sign of Steven. If he'd got out, as I thought, then where was he? Had he run off? And where had he got out? I couldn't understand it. And if the others were still hanging about on top of the shelters . . . that must mean they thought we were both down here. And if Steven was still down here, where was he? I thought I'd been through every square inch of this grotty place. And why was he keeping so quiet? He couldn't be hiding from me. He was supposed to find me.

I started to run down the main passage towards the end where the planks were, shouting "Steven, Steven." Now I was worried again, but this time not for myself. I was worried about him. Can you believe it – worried about what happened to Steven Taylor with his ferrety face and his nasty habits? Then I'd reached the planks and was banging on them again and shouting at the top of my voice.

But it was useless. I ought to know that. I knew where the others were. I'd seen them. They were up on top of the shelters, a good fifty yards away from where I was now. If they couldn't hear me from the ventilation shaft, they'd never hear me from here. There was nothing for it, I knew, but to go back and search the place to see if I could find Steven.

I was right back where I'd started – ages ago it seemed. Feeling my way along the passage wall, going carefully and slowly, wishing I had Ranji's fishing line to guide myself with. I began, without thinking, to count the steps – ten, eleven, twelve.

Just then, two things happened. My hand went off into empty space and I knew I was back by the side passage, where the dugout was, where I'd had my very own nightmare come true. And at the same time, my foot hit something, hard. I bent down.

It was Steven's torch, with the bulb smashed.

The Way Out

I held back a minute. Then I took two deep breaths and pushed my way back into the narrow, slimy gap in the wall. As I pushed through I could feel the wooden props crumbling and rotten under my fingers and the soil slithered down on my head and neck, making me flinch.

"Steven! Steven Taylor!"

"Mike!"

His voice sounded so close it shook me. It was close and far away if you know what I mean, because he was beneath me, in the dugout.

"What are you doing down there, Steven, you nit?"

"Doing, you idiot, I can't get out."

"Yes, you can," I shouted. "There's a table stuck

up by the wall. You can stand on it."

"That's what you think. It's all smashed up."

"Smashed up?"

"Yes. I fell on top of it when I came down. Hey Mike, help us up. I'm scared down here."

"I don't blame you, mate," I said. "I've been down there myself. It's like something out of a horror movie."

"Thanks very much. You make me feel a lot better. Now get me out will you."

I crouched down on the edge of the hole and felt round with my hands. There was nothing.

"Stretch your hands out, Steven."

"I am doing. I can't feel anything."

I got down on my stomach now and stretched out my hands again. They hit Steven's and he grabbed my wrist.

"Hold on. Where's your other hand."

We gripped one another's wrists as tight as we could. I could hear Steven scrabbling about in the dark underneath me. The strain on my arms was fantastic. The skin on my wrists was sore. I tried to shift backwards. I could hear him slipping.

"I can't make it, Mike."

"Come on." I got on to my knees and yanked as hard as I could.

The next thing I knew he was tumbling all over

me. I got one of his feet in my face. We struggled all over each other in the passage, treading on each other's fingers, pulling at each other's clothes. But he was up and he was safe.

A couple of minutes later we were sitting by the planks that covered the entrance . . . We both got our breath back and spoke at the same time.

"Hey, where did you get to?"

"What d'you mean, where did *I* get to? I was looking for you."

I told Steven what happened when I first fell into the hole.

"That's where you were," he said. "I thought you were farther off down the passage. I went up and down the main passage twice, then I got into those side tunnels and couldn't find my way."

"But, didn't you hear me shouting?"

"Oh ah. But I couldn't make out where you were."

"But, how did you come to fall down this hole?"

"Well, when I got back to the planks here and couldn't find you, that side passage was the only one I hadn't looked in. But just when I was going into it, my torch slipped out of my hand."

"I've got it here. It's broken."

"Oh heck. It's our Sam's. He'll kill me."

"Your Sam's a nasty piece of work," I said. The

words came out so quickly I was surprised. But he wasn't upset.

"I know he is. Hey, Mike, you know, he put me up to it."

"Up to what?"

"Having a fight with you."

"Get off."

"It's true an' all. I didn't want to. It didn't half hurt when we hit our hands together that day in the school yard."

"It did an' all." We both started laughing.

We didn't say anything for a while. I felt tired and a bit battered. But, you know, I was beginning to feel good. I remembered my peanut butter sandwich. I pulled it out of my pocket, chocolate bar, bits of grit and all and offered Steven half.

"Ta. Want a drink?"

"Not much. What've you got?"

"Coke."

He passed something to me and I put it to my lips. It tasted rubbery.

"What's this?"

"Hot water bottle. I stuck it up my jumper so you wouldn't see when we went down."

"You twister."

"Well you had a sandwich, didn't you."

"Oh all right, we both cheated. Hope they'll

come soon. I'm choked with this place."

"Right on. I bet we've been here two hours."

"At least."

"Hey, Mike, it was creepy down that hole, wasn't it. All those things down there."

"Yes, my Granddad reckons somebody was caught down here in an air raid during the war. It put the wind right up me. Hey, maybe your Granddad knows about it. He was in charge of these shelters, wasn't he?"

"Not much," Steven said. "You know our Sam's a rotten liar. Granddad wasn't in charge. He was just an air raid warden."

"Nothing wrong with that, is there?"

"Oh, I know. It's just our Sam. He's always talking big."

Just then, we heard a scraping noise behind us, some bumping and banging and creaking. Light showed between the planks and the wall.

Sam Taylor shouted: "Come on out. You've had twenty minutes."

We both shouted back. "Twenty minutes, nothing. It's been two hours at least."

I looked at my watch. I couldn't believe my eyes. It was not quite half past ten. Twenty minutes, I thought. I never want another twenty minutes like that again, ever. We struggled out on our hands and knees, bruised and mucky, blinking in the sunlight that hurt our eyes.

"Hey up," yelled Spotty Sam. "Our kid won. He found Baxter."

"No I didn't," Steven started to say. "It was . . ."
I interrupted.

"It was a draw."

"That's it," said Steven. "It was a draw."

12

Granddad Comes Clean

Ten minutes later we were out on the top and walking down the main road. Everybody agreed it was a draw. And when they heard what had happened to Steven and me, they all agreed we'd keep quiet about what we had done. We stopped at Nick's Caff on the way home and Sam bought coke for everyone. It was all done to go over big with Sandra but she took no notice. Spotty Sam's a pain and nothing can change that.

Then we drifted home. I was in luck, because Mum was out. I had a quick shower and craftily washed out my jeans and jumper and hung them out to dry. She saw them but didn't say anything when we had dinner. She couldn't say anything, anyway, because she's always going on about me keeping my things clean. But I think she had her own ideas.

That night Gran and Granddad came round again. I waited my chance for a talk with him. It took some doing because Dad and Mum kept interrupting just when I got a good conversation going. But in the end Gran and Mum went into the other room and Dad went out to the off-licence. Our Sis was out for the evening with a bloke from the library, "taking stock" as our Dad says when he wants to annoy her. So I had Granddad to myself for ten minutes. I asked him right out.

"Hey, Granddad, what's it like working underground?"

He stared at me.

"What d'you want to know for, lad? Listen, I made up my mind nobody else in this family's going down the pit. I made sure your mother married a railwayman." He started to laugh and then stopped again. "And your Dad wants you in college, you know."

"Oh, I know, Granddad. I'm just asking. Did you get used to it, all those times you were underground?"

He looked out of the window and said nothing for a while.

"I must have gone down that hole nearly ten thousand times, before I packed it in. I'll tell you something, Mike. I liked it less the last time, than I did the first . . ."

His voice died away.

"Hey, Granddad. You all right?"

"Eh, Mike. Oh ah. You know every time that cage went down, my stomach used to come up in my gullet. It never changed."

"I know what you mean, Granddad."

He stared at me.

"I believe you do, Mike."

"Granddad," I said a minute later. "Talking about being underground, you know those shelters off the main road?"

"What about them?"

"Did you ever go down them during the war? I mean when they were dropping bombs."

"You what, Mike?" He started to laugh. For a moment I thought he was going to start coughing, and that would bring our Gran in. But he stopped.

"You know what, Mike, *nobody* went down those shelters during the air raids."

"Hey, why?"

"Because they were not safe, lad, that's why. They were only dug to make people feel safe. But nobody trusted them. Death traps, those places."

"What did people do, then, Granddad?"

"Well, some went in that big cellar, under the

Co-op warehouse. That was safe enough. Six feet of concrete over it. And some went into a big basement they had under the biscuit factory. But most people stayed at home."

"Stayed at home."

"Oh ah. It wasn't like Liverpool or Sheffield, you know, Mike. There weren't all that many bombs and people thought it was a bit more dignified to stay in bed or come down in the kitchen for a cup of tea than jump into a smelly old hole in the ground. They used to say – 'If it's got my name on it it'll get me.' It sounds daft, I know, but that's how people feel."

"Is that how you felt when you were working underground, Granddad?"

"In a way, I suppose, Mike. After all, somebody had to go down there."

"Hey, Granddad. You said no one went down those shelters. But how about that bloke you said was trapped down there?"

"You hear too much for your own good."

"Come on Granddad. You said he'd had it when the bombs started dropping."

"Don't know what you're talking about, Mike."

"Oh, Granddad, stop messing about."

"Don't you be rude to your Granddad," Mum shouted from the next room. She can hear a pin drop at two hundred yards. But I had to know about that bloke in the shelters. I had to.

"Granddad . . ." I said.

He grinned. "You mean old Arthur Taylor."

"Taylor?"

"That's right. The Taylors who live on Crown Hill Estate."

"But Spotty Sam's Granddad's still alive."

"What's that? Of course he is. Who said different?"

"You said he got caught down the shelters and he'd had it."

"I never."

"You did."

"Oh, I know what you mean, lad." Granddad started to laugh again and his face got red. He gasped for breath.

"Arthur Taylor was an air raid warden. Big headed bloke he was. Well, this time, he went in the pub one afternoon, coming off early turn. He got so tanked up he didn't know what he was doing. So he landed up in the air raid post they had down the shelters."

"Like a dugout?" I asked.

He stared at me.

"I suppose so. He got half undressed and went to sleep. Then the raid started and the bombs woke him up. That place must have shook like an earthquake. He jumped up in a panic and rushed out in the street, shouting. Must have had a nightmare. Anyway he was the laughing stock of the town."

"Why?"

"Why? He left his trousers down there, along with his tin hat and his other gear, that's why."

"Tin hat?"

"His steel helmet."

Steel helmet. Then I knew what that weird old basin thing was, and those rotting old clothes on the ground in that hole. I started to laugh. Granddad joined in and just then Dad came in from the off-licence with some beer for Granddad.

"What are you two laughing about?"

"Just something that happened down the shelters, Dad."

He frowned.

"Shelters? Listen, Mike, you just keep away from those shelters. They're not safe. They're a death trap. Understand?"

He's telling me!

13

The Best of Friends

I was late to school again on Monday and was rushing in with the crowd at the main gate when I ran into someone. I mean I really ran into him. He got hold of my collar and twisted it so I nearly choked.

What a start to the week! It was Spotty Sam, of course. With him were Gary Wilson and Steven. Sam Taylor looked in a real, bad mood. But Steve grinned at me.

"Take no notice of him, Mike. He's dead worried."

"What for, Steve?"

"He wants Sandra whatsit to go to the disco with him on Friday and he doesn't know if she will or not."

He turned to Sam. I could see he was needling his

big brother, getting his own back.

"Hey, why don't you ask Mike to take a message for you. Sandra'll do anything for him."

Sam looked at me. He didn't know what to say. I started to edge away. When I was about ten yards in front of them, I called.

"She'd love to go to the disco with Sam. She says it'd give her a big thrill . . ."

I walked on a bit, then added,

". . . like dancing with Dracula."

Sam looked choked. He shouted to Steven who was nearer to me.

"Hey, our kid. You never really thumped him the other day. Just do it now, will you?"

Steve turned round.

"What, Mike? No, he's all right."

All these books are available at your local bookshop or newsagent, or can be ordered from the publishers.

To order direct from the publishers just tick the titles you want and fill in the form below:

Name ____

Address ____

____

Send to: Collins Children's Cash Sales
         PO Box 11
         Falmouth
         Cornwall
         TR10 9EN

Please enclose a cheque or postal order or debit my Visa/Access –

Credit card no:

Expiry date:

Signature:

– to the value of the cover price plus:

UK: 80p for the first book, and 20p per copy for each additional book ordered to a maximum charge of £2.00.

BFPO: 80p for the first book, and 20p per copy for each additional book.

Overseas and Eire: £1.50 for the first book, £1.00 for the second book, thereafter 30p per book.

Young Lions